Bratty Brothers and Selfish Sisters

All About Sibling Rivalry

Written and Illustrated by
R.W. Alley

Abbey Press
St. Meinrad, IN 47577

For Cassie and Max, sister and brother

Text © 2007 R.W. Alley
Illustrations © 2007 Saint Meinrad Archabbey
Published by One Caring Place
Abbey Press
St. Meinrad, Indiana 47577

Library of Congress Catalog Number
2006910145

ISBN 978-0-87029-404-4

Printed in the United States of America

A Message to Parents, Teachers, and Other Caring Adults

If you've picked up this book, it's probably safe to assume that you have more than one child. You might have two, or three, or more. Maybe they're all boys. Maybe they're all girls. Or, maybe they're a combination of both. They might be close in age. Their ages might be far apart.

But, no matter the number, gender, or age of the children in your family, they share one very, very important thing—YOU. And, as we all know, sharing anything can be hard sometimes. And when it comes to sharing people—like parents, for instance—things can get downright nasty.

Your children will always be rivals, to some degree, for your love and attention. Whether they are toddlers or teens, they will judge their own worth by how you allocate your attention between them and their siblings. It's a delicate balancing act, isn't it? Sometimes you may truly *like* one child's behavior better than the other's. But, you know that doesn't mean you *love* one more than the other. It is especially important at those times to show your equal love for both (or all).

Sibling rivalry is not a passing phase. Sibling rivalry is forever. Sometimes it can look pretty ugly and brothers and sisters can be awfully mean to each other, especially when they are young. However, by reassuring each child of his or her own special place in your heart, you encourage siblings to grow together, not apart. You also encourage them to find their own special place in the family. That leads to their finding their own special place in the world. And what is the world, after all, but one very large family?

—R.W. Alley

What's a Sibling?

If you have a sibling, it means you have a brother or a sister. Maybe more than one brother or sister. Or, maybe no brothers and only a sister. Or sisters. There are lots of combinations. But, you get the idea.

Having a sibling also means that there's almost always another kid around the house. It's like having a built-in playmate: Someone to share games with; someone to share secrets with; someone to share the really big popcorn with at the movies.

Does all this sharing mean that you and your sibling are best friends?

Not always.

Sharing Things Is Hard

Sometimes things are hard to share. When you and your sibling want the same thing, and only one of you can have it, you and your sibling are having a rivalry. Grown-ups call this "sibling rivalry." You may call it really, really annoying.

The new bunk bed is here! You've been planning all the things you'd do with the top bunk. But, your brother asked for the top bunk first, so he gets it. Bunk beds are hard to share.

It's a long, hot afternoon and suddenly you have a great idea. "Time to pogo stick," you announce. "Me first, me first," says your little sister. "My idea, so I go first," you say. Your little sister hollers. "It's not nice to make your little sister holler," says your big sister. Then she hops on the pogo stick and hops away. Pogo sticks are hard to share.

Sharing People Is Really Hard

Often, the hardest thing to share is people. Usually, the hardest people for siblings to share are your parents.

You've been working on a new dance all morning. You want to show Mom, but she says, "We have to take your brother to tuba lessons. Later, OK?" Maybe you can show her while his lesson is going on. "Not here, dear. Later, OK?"

Back home, you say, "Look at my dance now, Mom!" But everyone has to eat before your brother's recital. Mom says, "Later, dear, OK?"

Who cares about the recital? You have something special to show. It's not fair.

When Is It Fair to Share?

Just because it's your brother's recital, he got his favorite dinner. Now you're sitting between Mom and Grandpa, listening to the music. You're practicing your dance in your seat. "Shhh," Grandpa whispers, "you have to sit still." Grandpa doesn't know you have a new dance. Everyone is just listening to your brother and his tuba.

Sitting there, you begin to listen, too. It's not bad. Your feet like the music. Everyone claps at the end. When you get home, you ask your brother to play his tuba while you show your dance to everyone.

You do your best dance ever, and everybody claps at the end.

How Old Are You?

How old you are has a lot to do with the rivalry you feel. If you're the oldest, you can probably do more than your siblings. But that won't always mean you'll get more attention.

Look at that great block castle you've made, with bridges, windows, and roads. You've cut out flags and made paper people. Dad gets out his camera. "Don't forget the drawbridge," you say.

But, Dad's not taking a picture of your castle. He's saying, "Look at that! The baby has stacked two whole blocks!"

Unbelievable! Somehow your foot slips and baby's blocks fall over.

Being the Oldest Takes Patience

Remember when you were little and how you made block towers? Dad took lots of pictures then, too.

You hand your brother some blocks. "I'm sorry I knocked over your tower," you say. "Show me how you built it." He sticks his teeth into the blocks, getting them all gooey. It helps the blocks stick together.

"Look at that," you say. "You've stacked three blocks all by yourself."

Dad takes a picture of the tower and your castle. Then, your brother's foot slips and your castle tumbles down. Sometimes you have to be careful what you teach a younger sibling.

You're the Baby

If you're the youngest, it can feel like you aren't good at anything when you're around your older sibling. Even something simple, like kicking a ball.

"Pick me, pick me," you shout. But, whenever you play soccer with your sister's friends, you get picked last. "Pass it to me. Pass it to me," you shout. No one does. Everyone passes to your sister.

But instead of hoping she'll trip and fall in the mud, maybe you could ask her to teach you to play better. So when you're playing with your friends and yell, "Pass me the ball," they do.

You're in the Middle

If you have both older and younger siblings, then you're in the middle. It's easy to feel lost there. Sometimes you just have to speak up.

You're home from school and there's a good test paper in your backpack. But, as soon as you get in the door, Mom says, "Isn't it wonderful, your little sister spelled 'dog' with the 'fridge letters." Then your older brother says, "Mom, I'm going to be in the county spelling bee!"

Maybe you think no one cares what you have in your backpack. But, really they just don't know. So, show them.

Who's the Best?

No matter who's older, having a sibling means that sometimes you have to show you're braver, or stronger, or smarter.

You're at the edge of the lake. The water is dark. You see bubbles from fish popping on the surface. "I'll race you to the float," you say.

"OK," says your sibling. "I'll even give you a head start. You go in first."

After an hour or so, it starts to get dark and a chilly breeze brings the sound of Mom calling you both in. Later, you wonder what kind of man-eating fish made the bubbles in the lake.

A Special Sibling

Suppose your sibling needs to be treated in a special way. Maybe there are a bunch of trips to the doctor. Your sibling likely will need lots of extra help from Mom and Dad.

You might find yourself thinking, "I wish my sister was more like regular kids." Or, "If my brother was normal, Mom could spend more time with me." Don't feel guilty for thinking these thoughts. They don't mean you love your sibling less. It's only that you wish things were easier for everyone in the family.

Think of things you can do to help. Suggest things you can do together as a family.

The Talented Sibling

What happens if your sibling has a special ability that everyone makes a big deal over?

You were on the tennis team first. You worked really hard to just get to seventh place on the team. Then one day the coach says, "Hey look at your brother's backhand. I can't believe he only started playing tennis last month. I think he should play at number one in the first match of the season."

"Maybe I should just make my racquet into a snowshoe," you think.

Looking Inside

It's time to look deep inside for your unique talents. Remember, not everyone needs cheering crowds.

Maybe you'd rather stay home, drawing superheroes, but you have to go to your sister's swim meet. Everyone cheers for her. You think no one cares if you're there or not. But your sister is glad you're there.

So you draw her on the corner of the program. "That looks just like her!" says Dad. You cheer your sister and her teammates as you draw their splashes and dives.

Now, you have a pocketful of drawings of your new superhero, Captain Fish. You cheer quietly for yourself all the way home.

I Told You So

Making cookies seemed like a good idea. Who doesn't like cookies? However, things got pretty messy and the stove didn't work right. And your sister saw the whole thing. "I knew you'd make a big mess," she says. "I told you so."

Dad says, "What were you thinking? Your sister wouldn't make a mess like this!" Mom says, "Your sister is so neat. You're so messy. I've never seen such different children."

It's lonely in your room when your parents are disappointed with you. You wonder, "Do Mom and Dad love my sister more because she's neater?"

Not a chance.

You're Always Loved

Whether you're the oldest, youngest, or somewhere in the middle, you have a special place in your family. Your family wouldn't be complete without you.

Families are like puzzles—sometimes very complicated puzzles. It's not surprising if you get jealous when someone else's piece fits in more easily than yours. But, the shape of the puzzle's pieces change as your family changes. And, sometimes your piece will fit in more easily than your siblings.

Yet, brothers and sisters are forever. So, while sometimes you may stick out your tongue at your sibling, other times you might just say, "You know, these cookies aren't half bad."

R.W. Alley has illustrated more than a hundred books for children, including the popular *Pearl and Wagner* and *Detective Dinosaur* books. He has both written and illustrated another half dozen other titles, including the Elf-help Book for Kids *Making a Boring Day Better*. He also has illustrated all of Abbey's Elf-help Therapy books.

Mr. Alley lives in Barrington, Rhode Island, with his wife and two children. During the school year, he often visits local elementary school classrooms, to talk and draw about how words and pictures come together to become the books that the children read. He might try out a new story on a class. And he always listens very carefully to the children's suggestions. You can check out his work at his website: www.rwalley.com.